WAITING FOR THE

Great Pumpkin

YES, SIR.. THIS PAMPHLET TELLS YOU ALL ABOUT THE "GREAT PUMPKIN"... I THINK YOU'LL REALLY LIKE IT...
I'LL BET HE DIDN'T EVEN READ IT..
10-29
SCHULZ

WAITING FOR THE Great Pumpkin

CHARLES M. SCHULZ

FANTAGRAPHICS BOOKS, SEATTLE

You Believe in Santa Claus and I'll Believe in the Great Pumpkin!

10-26
WHAT IN THE WORLD ARE YOU DOING?
DON'T YOU KNOW?
THIS IS THE TIME OF YEAR WHEN WE ALL WRITE TO THE "GREAT PUMPKIN," AND TELL HIM WHAT WE WANT FOR HALLOWEEN
THE "GREAT PUMPKIN" LOVES LITTLE CHILDREN
I CAN SEE HIM NOW RISING UP OUT OF THE PUMPKIN PATCH WITH HIS BIG BAG OF TOYS!
SCHULZ

HALLOWEEN'S COMING, CHARLIE BROWN!

I'VE WRITTEN A LETTER TO THE "GREAT PUMPKIN" TELLING HIM WHAT I WANT HIM TO BRING ME...
10-27

IF YOU HAVEN'T WRITTEN TO HIM YET, CHARLIE BROWN, YOU'D BETTER HURRY!

OH, I LOVE THIS TIME OF YEAR! EVERYONE'S SO FULL OF JOY AND GOOD WILL!
SCHULZ

10-28

WHY DON'T WE GET THE WHOLE GANG TOGETHER, AND GO OUT AND SING PUMPKIN CAROLS?
SCHULZ

...AND THEN ON HALLOWEEN NIGHT THE "GREAT PUMPKIN" RISES UP OUT OF THE PUMPKIN PATCH...
..AND HE BRINGS TOYS TO ALL THE GOOD LITTLE CHILDREN IN THE WORLD!
YOU'RE CRAZY!
ALL RIGHT, SO YOU BELIEVE IN SANTA CLAUS, AND I'LL BELIEVE IN THE "GREAT PUMPKIN"..
10-29
THE WAY I SEE IT, IT DOESN'T MATTER WHAT YOU BELIEVE JUST SO YOU'RE SINCERE!
SCHULZ

TOMORROW NIGHT IS OUR BIG NIGHT, LINUS..

ALL YOU HAVE TO DO IS WALK UP TO A HOUSE, RING THE DOORBELL AND SAY, "TRICKS OR TREATS!"

ARE YOU SURE THAT'S LEGAL?
OF COURSE, IT'S LEGAL!
10-30

GOOD... I WOULDN'T WANT TO BE ACCUSED OF TAKING PART IN A RUMBLE!
SCHULZ

WELL, WHAT'S THE MATTER WITH **YOU**?

YOU DIDN'T **TELL** ME YOU WERE GOING TO **KILL** IT!
10-31
SCHULZ

WELL, HALLOWEEN HAS COME AND GONE...

SO IT HAS

DID THE "GREAT PUMPKIN" BRING YOU LOTS OF NICE PRESENTS?

OH, SHUT UP!
11-2
SCHULZ

LOOK AT ME.. I'M THE "GREAT PUMPKIN"!

I RISE UP OUT OF THE PUMPKIN PATCH, AND BRING TOYS TO ALL THE CHILDREN ON HALLOWEEN!

HEY, LINUS! HOW MANY TOYS DID HE BRING YOU?!!
HAHAHAHA!!!

I WAS A VICTIM OF FALSE DOCTRINE..
11-3
SCHULZ

ARE YOU THE "GREAT PUMPKIN"?

NO, I'M YOUR KID BROTHER WITH A SHEET OVER MY HEAD..

Santa Claus vs. the Great Pumpkin

THIS IS NO TIME TO BE DEPRESSED, CHARLIE BROWN...
10-20
THIS IS THE SEASON TO BE JOLLY...
IN LESS THAN TWO WEEKS, HE'LL BE COMING!
WHO?
THE GREAT PUMPKIN!
OH, GOOD GRIEF!
SCHULZ

LUCY DOESN'T BELIEVE IN THE GREAT PUMPKIN..

SHE DOESN'T BELIEVE THAT ON HALLOWEEN NIGHT HE RISES OUT OF THE PUMPKIN PATCH WITH HIS BAG OF TOYS FOR ALL THE GOOD LITTLE CHILDREN OF THE WORLD

LUCY DOESN'T BELIEVE **THAT**?
NO...
10/21

I CAN'T IMAGINE WHAT HAS MADE HER SO BLIND!
SCHULZ

DON'T START IN WITH THAT "GREAT PUMPKIN" BUSINESS AGAIN, DO YOU HEAR ME?
IT'S THE MOST STUPID THING I'VE EVER HEARD OF! IT'S STUPID, STUPID, STUPID!!
10-22
YOU HAVE JUST OFFENDED ONE OF CHILDHOOD'S MOST CHERISHED BELIEFS!
SCHULZ

ALL OVER THE WORLD CHILDREN ARE WRITING LETTERS TO THE "GREAT PUMPKIN"

THIS IS BECAUSE ON HALLOWEEN NIGHT HE RISES OUT OF THE PUMPKIN PATCH, AND **FLIES** THROUGH THE AIR WITH A BIG BAG FULL OF TOYS!

SO IF YOU'RE A **GOOD** LITTLE GIRL, SALLY, HE'LL BRING **YOU** SOMETHING, TOO!

SUDDENLY I FEEL LIKE I'VE HEARD EVERYTHING!
SCHULZ
10-24

THE WHOLE TROUBLE WITH YOU IS YOU'VE GOT THIS 'GREAT PUMPKIN' MIXED UP WITH SANTA CLAUS!

I HAVE NOT! THEY'RE TWO DISTINCT PERSONALITIES!
ALL RIGHT, THEN! TELL ME THE DIFFERENCE! GO AHEAD! TELL ME!

WITH SANTA CLAUS IT'S JUST A JOB! HE GIVES AWAY ALL THOSE TOYS BECAUSE IT'S EXPECTED OF HIM!

THE GREAT PUMPKIN GIVES AWAY HIS TOYS BECAUSE HE FEELS HE'S FULFILLING A MORAL OBLIGATION!!
OH, GOOD GRIEF!
SCHULZ
10-25

ALL RIGHT, SO WE WRITE A LETTER TO THE GREAT PUMPKIN TELLING HIM WHAT WE WANT HIM TO BRING US...

WHERE DO WE SEND IT?

TO THE "GREAT PUMPKIN", IN CARE OF "THE PUMPKIN PATCH".....WHERE ELSE?

WHERE ELSE, INDEED?
10-26
SCHULZ

TO: THE GREAT PUMPKIN
C/O THE PUMPKIN PATCH

I DON'T SEE HOW THIS IS EVER GOING TO GET DELIVERED...

I'M SURPRISED AT YOU, CHARLIE BROWN!
10-27

YOUR LACK OF CONFIDENCE IN OUR POSTAL DEPARTMENT IS AN INSULT TO THE ENTIRE ORGANIZATION!
U.S. MAIL
SCHULZ

IF THERE'S A "GREAT PUMPKIN," HOW COME NOBODY HAS EVER SEEN HIM?

HUH? HOW COME? ANSWER ME THAT! HOW COME NOBODY HAS EVER SEEN HIM? HUH? NYAHH! NYAHH! NYAHH!!

I REFUSE TO ARGUE WITH YOU BECAUSE YOU'RE BECOMING VERY OBNOXIOUS....
10-28

BIG-SISTERWISE, THAT IS!
SCHULZ

SANTA CLAUS IS **TWICE** THE MAN THE GREAT PUMPKIN IS!

YOU'RE CRAZY!
THE GREAT PUMPKIN DOESN'T EVEN **EXIST**!

WHY DON'T YOU KEEP QUIET? YOU DON'T EVEN KNOW WHAT YOU'RE TALKING ABOUT!
WELL, YOU'RE SO STUPID, YOU BELIEVE **ANYTHING**!

I'M ALWAYS DISTURBED BY DENOMINATIONAL SQUABBLING
10-29
SCHULZ

IF ANYONE HAD TOLD ME I'D BE OUT CRAWLING AROUND AMONG A BUNCH OF PUMPKINS ON HALLOWEEN NIGHT, I'D HAVE SAID THEY WERE CRAZY!

THIS IS FAR ENOUGH..

JUST THINK, CHARLIE BROWN... WHEN THE "GREAT PUMPKIN" RISES OUT OF THE PUMPKIN PATCH, WE'LL BE HERE TO SEE HIM!

IT JUST OCCURRED TO ME THAT THERE MUST BE TEN MILLION PUMPKIN PATCHES IN THIS COUNTRY.. WHAT MAKES YOU THINK WE'RE IN THE RIGHT ONE?

JUST A FEELING I HAVE, CHARLIE BROWN, ALTHOUGH I THINK THIS MUST BE THE KIND OF PUMPKIN PATCH HE WOULD PREFER...

I DOUBT IF HE LIKES LARGE PUMPKIN PATCHES...THEY'RE TOO COMMERCIAL..HE LIKES SMALL HOMEY ONES...THEY'RE MORE SINCERE...
SOMEHOW I'VE NEVER THOUGHT OF A PUMPKIN PATCH AS BEING SINCERE...

THERE HE IS! THERE HE IS!

IT'S THE 'GREAT PUMPKIN'! HE'S RISING UP OUT OF THE PUMPKIN PATCH
OH H H
KLUNK
WHAT HAPPENED? DID I FAINT? WHAT DID HE LEAVE US? DID HE LEAVE US ANY TOYS?
NO TOYS... JUST A USED DOG...
HE MUST BE WELL ON HIS WAY BY THIS TIME.. HAPPY JOURNEY, O, GREAT PUMPKIN! HAPPY JOURNEY!
"USED DOG"! GOOD GRIEF!
SCHULZ

GOOD-BY, 'TIL NEXT YEAR, O, GREAT PUMPKIN!
FAREWELL, FAREWELL, FAREWELL! THANKS FOR EVERYTHING!
SCHULZ 10-31
SIGH WHO AM I KIDDING?

I BELIEVED IN THE "GREAT PUMPKIN"! I REALLY DID!

I BELIEVED IN THE "GREAT PUMPKIN" WITH EVERY FIBER OF MY BEING!

11-1
RATS!

IN ALL THIS WORLD THERE IS NOTHING MORE UPSETTING THAN THE CLOBBERING OF A CHERISHED BELIEF!
TRUE!
SCHULZ

I THOUGHT FOR SURE THERE WAS A "GREAT PUMPKIN"

HOW COULD I HAVE BEEN SO STUPID?
DON'T LET IT BOTHER YOU, LINUS...

WE ALL DO THINGS NOW AND THEN THAT MAKE US LOSE CONFIDENCE IN OURSELVES... EVERYONE DOES...
11-2

WELL, ALMOST EVERYONE!
SCHULZ

WHAT'S THE CURE FOR DISILLUSIONMENT, CHARLIE BROWN?

A CHOCOLATE-CREAM AND A FRIENDLY PAT ON THE BACK

SCHULZ
GOOD OL' CHARLIE BROWN!
11-3

NOW, WOULD YOU CARE TO READ SOME LITERATURE I'VE PREPARED ABOUT THE "GREAT PUMPKIN"?
GET A
WHEN THE "GR

Oh, Great Pumpkin, You're Going to Drive Me Crazy!

DEAR GREAT PUMPKIN, HOW HAVE YOU BEEN?
10-23

WE ARE LOOKING FORWARD TO YOUR COMING ON HALLOWEEN NIGHT WITH YOUR BAG FULL OF PRESENTS. I HAVE TRIED TO BE A GOOD BOY ALL YEAR.

HAVE YOU NOTICED?
SCHULZ

..AND THEN, SALLY, ON HALLOWEEN NIGHT, THE GREAT PUMPKIN APPEARS!

HE FLIES THROUGH THE AIR, AND BRINGS TOYS TO ALL THE CHILDREN OF THE WORLD!

HA!

10-24
I DON'T THINK SHE BELIEVED ME...
SCHULZ

YOU'RE CRAZY! YOU'RE JUST PLAIN STUPID CRAZY!

YOU TALK LIKE SOMEONE WHO'S JUST FALLEN OUT OF A TREE! YOU'RE STARK RAVING STUPID!!
10-25

I SHOULD HAVE KNOWN BETTER...

THERE ARE THREE THINGS I HAVE LEARNED NEVER TO DISCUSS WITH PEOPLE...RELIGION, POLITICS AND THE GREAT PUMPKIN!
SCHULZ

YOU'RE AT IT AGAIN, AREN'T YOU?

"THE GREAT PUMPKIN RISES OUT OF THE PUMPKIN PATCH ON HALLOWEEN NIGHT, AND FLIES THROUGH THE AIR!" GOOD GRIEF!
10-26

HOW CAN YOU **BELIEVE** THAT?
I **HAVE** TO BELIEVE IT...I'VE ALREADY SENT OUT FIFTY-SEVEN PUMPKIN CARDS...

IT WOULD BE ECONOMICALLY DISASTROUS FOR ME **NOT** TO BELIEVE IT!
SCHULZ

WHAT ARE YOU DOING OUT HERE?
I'M WAITING FOR THE "GREAT PUMPKIN" TO APPEAR

YOU HAVE A LONG WAIT... HALLOWEEN ISN'T UNTIL NEXT TUESDAY..
I DON'T CARE.. IT'S VERY PEACEFUL OUT HERE...

10-27

MOST PSYCHIATRISTS AGREE THAT SITTING IN A PUMPKIN PATCH IS EXCELLENT THERAPY FOR A TROUBLED MIND!
SCHULZ

YOU'RE **CRAZY**! YOU'RE COMPLETELY OUT OF YOUR MIND!

YOU JUST DON'T UNDERSTAND..
UNDERSTAND?! **HA!** I UNDERSTAND THAT YOU'RE **CRACKING UP**!

ANYONE WHO WOULD SIT OUT IN A PUMPKIN PATCH FOR FIVE DAYS WAITING FOR THE "GREAT PUMPKIN" TO ARRIVE IS ABSOLUTELY **CRAZY**!

10-28
SCHULZ

EACH YEAR THE "GREAT PUMPKIN" RISES OUT OF THE PUMPKIN PATCH THAT HE THINKS IS THE MOST SINCERE

HE'S GOT TO PICK THIS ONE! HE'S **GOT** TO! I DON'T SEE HOW A PUMPKIN PATCH CAN BE MORE SINCERE THAN THIS ONE!

YOU CAN LOOK ALL AROUND AND THERE'S NOT A SIGN OF HYPOCRISY'...
10-30

NOTHING BUT SINCERITY AS FAR AS THE EYE CAN SEE!
SCHULZ

ISN'T LINUS GOING OUT FOR "TRICKS OR TREATS"?
NO, HE'S SITTING IN THE PUMPKIN PATCH WAITING FOR THE GREAT PUMPKIN TO APPEAR
10-31

WELL, WHEN YOU GO UP TO THIS NEXT HOUSE, ASK THE LADY FOR AN EXTRA TREAT FOR YOUR LITTLE BROTHER WHO IS SITTING OUT IN THE PUMPKIN PATCH

ALL I GOT FROM HER WAS A VERY PECULIAR LOOK!
SCHULZ

HEY, WAKE UP... HALLOWEEN IS OVER..YOU MISSED THE GREAT PUMPKIN!

IT JUST CAME OVER THE RADIO..HE APPEARED IN A VERY SINCERE PUMPKIN PATCH OWNED BY SOMEONE NAMED FREEMAN IN NEW JERSEY!

11-1

OH, GREAT PUMPKIN, YOU'RE GOING TO DRIVE ME CRAZY!!!
SCHULZ

HA HA HA!

10-26

GREAT SECRETARY RISES FROM HER
K AND RIDES THROUGH THE CITY IN
AXICAB WITH NOTE PADS FOR ALL
SECRETARIES EVERYWHERE!
WAIT! LET ME TELL YOU
ABOUT MOTHER-IN-LAW'S

True Love Revealed in the Pumpkin Patch

DEAR GREAT PUMPKIN, I AM LOOKING FORWARD TO YOUR ARRIVAL ON HALLOWEEN NIGHT.
I HOPE YOU WILL BRING ME LOTS OF PRESENTS.
10-13
EVERYONE TELLS ME YOU ARE A FAKE, BUT I BELIEVE IN YOU.
SINCERELY, LINUS VAN PELT
P.S. IF YOU REALLY ARE A FAKE, DON'T TELL ME. I DON'T WANT TO KNOW.
SCHULZ

THIS IS THE TIME OF YEAR TO WRITE TO THE 'GREAT PUMPKIN'
ON HALLOWEEN NIGHT HE RISES OUT OF THE PUMPKIN PATCH, AND FLIES THROUGH THE AIR WITH HIS BAG OF TOYS FOR ALL THE CHILDREN!
I'M WRITING TO HIM NOW...DO YOU WANT ME TO PUT IN A GOOD WORD FOR YOU, CHARLIE BROWN?
10-16
BY ALL MEANS...I CAN USE ALL THE INFLUENCE I CAN GET IN HIGH PLACES!
SCHULZ

I'VE BEEN THINKING...

WHY COULDN'T I RUN OFF A FORM LETTER ON A STENCIL, AND SEND THE SAME LETTER TO THE 'GREAT PUMPKIN' SANTA CLAUS AND THE EASTER BUNNY?

I DON'T THINK THEY'D EVER KNOW THE DIFFERENCE.... I'M **SURE** THE 'GREAT PUMPKIN' WOULDN'T... HE'S VERY NAÏVE...
10-18

I WISH YOU HADN'T TOLD ME THAT... I'M DISILLUSIONED...
SCHULZ

YOU MEAN YOU'RE GOING TO SEND THE SAME FORM LETTER TO THE 'GREAT PUMPKIN', SANTA CLAUS AND THE EASTER BUNNY?

WHY NOT? THOSE GUYS GET SO MUCH MAIL THEY CAN'T POSSIBLY TELL THE DIFFERENCE...

I BET THEY DON'T EVEN READ THE LETTERS THEMSELVES! HOW COULD THEY?!
10-19

THE TROUBLE WITH YOU, CHARLIE BROWN, IS YOU DON'T UNDERSTAND HOW THESE BIG ORGANIZATIONS WORK!
SCHULZ

DEAR GREAT PUMPKIN, HALLOWEEN IS NOW ONLY A FEW DAYS AWAY.

CHILDREN ALL OVER THE WORLD AWAIT YOUR COMING.

I'M NOT AWAITING HIS COMING... I THINK HE'S A FAKE!
10-25

I'M GLAD YOU DIDN'T HEAR THAT.
SCHULZ

DEAR GREAT PUMPKIN, THIS WILL BE MY LAST LETTER TO YOU BEFORE HALLOWEEN.
WHEN YOU RISE OUT OF THE PUMPKIN PATCH THAT NIGHT, PLEASE REMEMBER I AM YOUR MOST LOYAL FOLLOWER.
HAVE A NICE TRIP.
10-26
DON'T FORGET TO TAKE OUT FLIGHT INSURANCE.
SCHULZ

AND ON HALLOWEEN NIGHT THE "GREAT PUMPKIN" RISES OUT OF THE PUMPKIN PATCH...
10-29

THEN HE FLIES THROUGH THE AIR TO BRING TOYS TO ALL THE GOOD LITTLE CHILDREN EVERYWHERE!

THAT'S A GOOD STORY...

I PLACE IT JUST A LITTLE BELOW THE ONE ABOUT THE FLYING REINDEER!
SCHULZ

YOU DON'T BELIEVE THE STORY OF THE "GREAT PUMPKIN"?
10-30

I'M DISILLUSIONED! I THOUGHT LITTLE GIRLS ALWAYS BELIEVED EVERYTHING THAT WAS TOLD TO THEM

I THOUGHT LITTLE GIRLS WERE INNOCENT AND TRUSTING...

WELCOME TO 1962!
SCHULZ

ALL RIGHT, SALLY...YOU WANT PROOF...YOU'RE GOING TO GET IT...
10-31

WE'LL JUST SIT HERE IN THIS PUMPKIN PATCH, AND YOU'LL SEE THE "GREAT PUMPKIN" WITH YOUR OWN EYES!

IF YOU TRY TO HOLD MY HAND, I'LL SLUG YOU!!
SCHULZ

HALLOWEEN IS OVER!! I'VE MISSED IT!!!

YOU BLOCKHEAD, YOU'VE KEPT ME UP ALL NIGHT WAITING FOR THE "GREAT PUMPKIN," AND HE NEVER CAME!

I DIDN'T GET A CHANCE TO GO OUT FOR "TRICKS OR TREATS"! IT WAS ALL YOUR FAULT!

I'LL SUE!!
SCHULZ

I WAS ROBBED!
I SPENT THE WHOLE NIGHT WAITING FOR THE "GREAT PUMPKIN" WHEN I COULD HAVE BEEN OUT FOR "TRICKS OR TREATS"
YOU'VE HEARD ABOUT FURY AND A WOMAN SCORNED, HAVEN'T YOU?
YES, I GUESS I HAVE...
11-2
WELL, THAT'S NOTHING COMPARED TO THE FURY OF A WOMAN WHO HAS BEEN CHEATED OUT OF "TRICKS OR TREATS"!
SCHULZ

WHAT A FOOL I WAS!

I COULD HAVE HAD CANDY AND APPLES AND GUM AND COOKIES AND MONEY AND ALL SORTS OF THINGS, BUT, NO! I HAD TO LISTEN TO YOU! WHAT A FOOL I WAS!

"TRICKS OR TREATS" COMES ONLY ONCE A YEAR, AND I MISS IT BY SITTING IN A PUMPKIN PATCH WITH A BLOCKHEAD!
11-3

YOU OWE ME RESTITUTION!!!
SCHULZ

I'M NOT SPEAKING TO YOU! AFTER WHAT HAPPENED ON HALLOWEEN NIGHT, I'M NEVER GOING TO SPEAK TO YOU AGAIN!
11-6
I WOULDN'T SPEAK TO YOU IF I MET YOU ON THE STREET, ON THE OCEAN, IN THE AIR OR ON THE MOON!
HOW ABOUT IF I WERE COMING THROUGH THE RYE?!
SCHULZ

YOUR SISTER'S NOT SPEAKING TO ME, CHARLIE BROWN..

YOU BET I'M NOT! BECAUSE OF HIM I MISSED GOING OUT FOR "TRICKS OR TREATS" ON HALLOWEEN! I'M NEVER GOING TO SPEAK TO HIM AGAIN AS LONG AS I LIVE!
11-7

MY LIFE IS RUINED...

IS IT ?!!
SCHULZ

SCHULZ
MOM! DAD! THERE'S A PUMPKIN THIEF IN OUR PUMPKIN PATCH!
NO, WAIT
A THIE
GOING T
THE "GREAT
WHEN H

YOU SEE, ON HALLOWEEN NIGHT THE "GREAT PUMPKIN" RISES OUT OF THE...
YOU
A PUM
HUH
-29
I DID IT! I GOT
I CA

ANT
KIN,
WUMP!

WAITING FOR THE GREAT PUMPKIN
Charles M. Schulz

Editor: Gary Groth
Designer: Jacob Covey
Associate Publisher: Eric Reynolds
Publisher: Gary Groth

Special thanks to Marcie Daniel for her invaluable assistance.

Waiting for the Great Pumpkin is copyright © 2014 Peanuts Worldwide LLC.
Permission to duplicate materials from *Peanuts* comic strips must be
obtained from Peanuts Worldwide.

Fantagraphics Books, 7563 Lake City Way NE, Seattle, WA 98115, USA. For a free
full-color catalog of comics, call 1-800-657-1100. Our books may be viewed
and purchased on our website at www.fantagraphics.com.

ISBN 978-1-60699-772-7
First printing: September 2014
Printed in China

Thanks to: Randall Bethune, Big Planet Comics, Black Hook Press of Japan, Nick Capetillo, Kevin Czapiewski, John DiBello, Juan Manuel Domínguez, Mathieu Doublet, Dan Evans III, Thomas Eykemans, Scott Fritsch-Hammes, Coco and Eddie Gorodetsky, Karen Green, Ted Haycraft, Eduardo Takeo "Lizarkeo" Igarashi, Nevdon Jamgochian, Andy Koopmans, Philip Nel, Vanessa Palacios, Kurt Sayenga, Anne Lise Rostgaard Schmidt, Christian Schremser, Secret Headquarters, Paul van Dijken, Mungo van Krimpen-Hall, Jason Aaron Wong, and Thomas Zimmermann